The Delta Is My Home

Ehdııtat shanankat t'agoonch'uu

Uvanga Nunatarmuitmi aimayuaqtunga

Fifth House Ltd.
A Fitzhenry & Whiteside Company
1511, 1800-4 St. SW
Calgary, Alberta T2S 2S5

1-800-387-9776
www.fitzhenry.ca

Ducks Unlimited Canada
Conserving Canada's Wetlands

CANADIAN NORTH
seriously northern

CIBC

Mixed Sources
Product group from well-managed
forests and other controlled sources
www.fsc.org Cert no. SW-COC-1271
© 1996 Forest Stewardship Council
FSC

First published in the
United States in 2008 by
Fitzhenry & Whiteside
311 Washington Street
Brighton, Massachusetts,
02135

Cover and interior design by John Luckhurst
Frontispiece map by Toby Foord
Photography by Tessa Macintosh
Additional photographs by Joe Benoit and Dave Jones, Gwich'in Tribal Council—Land Administration Staff (Mount Goodenough, p.2); Wayne Lynch (muskrats, p.13); John Poirer, Prince of Wales Northern Heritage Centre (muskrat push-up, p.13); Fleming/NWT Archives/N-1979-050-0092 (muskrat Sunday, p.15); Wayne Lynch (ducks, p.17)

Illustrations by Autumn Downey (Aklavik flag, printed by permission of the Hamlet of Aklavik, p.8; and reworkings of push-up illustration, pp.12-13)

Edited by Meaghan Craven
Proofread by Michelle Lomberg

The type in this book is set in 10-on-15 point Trebuchet Regular and 10-on-13 point Tekton Oblique.

The publisher gratefully acknowledges the support of The Canada Council for the Arts and the Department of Canadian Heritage.

We acknowledge the financial support of the Government of Canada through the Book Publishing Industry Development Program (BPIDP) for our publishing activities.

The authors would like to thank Canadian North, CIBC, Ducks Unlimited Canada, the Gwich'in Land Use Planning Board (GLUPB), the NWT Protected Areas Strategy Secretariat, and WWF-Canada for financial assistance in the completion of this book.

Printed in Canada by Friesens on Forest Stewardship Council (FSC) Approved paper

2008 / 1

Library and Archives Canada Cataloguing in Publication

McLeod, Tom
The delta is my home = Ehdiitat shanakat t'agoonch'uu Uvanga Nunatarmuitmi aimayuaqtunga / Tom McLeod and Mindy Willett; photographs by Tessa Macintosh.

(Land is our storybook) Includes text in Gwich'in and Inuvialuktun.

ISBN 978-1-897252-32-1

1. McLeod, Tom—Juvenile literature. 2. Mackenzie River Delta (N.W.T. and Yukon)—Juvenile literature. 3. Gwich'in Indians—Hunting—Juvenile literature. 4. Inuvialuit—Hunting--Juvenile literature. 5. Traditional ecological knowledge—Mackenzie River Delta (N.W.T. and Yukon)—Juvenile literature. 6. Aklavik (N.W.T.)—Biography—Juvenile literature. I. Willett, Mindy, 1968- II. Title. III. Series.

E99.K84M35 2008   j971.9'300497120092   C2008-900420-5

Acknowledgements

We would like to thank: Shannon Haszard and Alicia Korpach of Ducks Unlimited Canada, Susan Mackenzie (land use planner) and the Gwich'in Land Use Planning Board, Pete Ewins and Freya Nales of WWF-Canada, Miki Ehrlich, Kris Johnson and Karen Hamre of the NWT Protected Areas Strategy Secretariat, and CIBC for their financial contributions; the community of Aklavik for their hospitality; Alestine Andre and William Firth of the Gwich'in Social and Cultural Institute for translations; Judith Drinnan of the Yellowknife Book Cellar for her ongoing encouragement and support of northern authors; Wayne Lynch for his wildlife photography; John Stewart and Gladys Norwegian of the GNWT Department of Education, Culture and Employment for the translations of the traditional stories and for reviewing the books; Tom Andrews of the Prince of Wales Heritage Centre and Ingrid Kritsch and Alestine Andre of the Gwich'in Social and Cultural Institute for reviewing the book; Autumn Downey for reworking Tom's drawings; Gladys Edwards, Sarah Poloquin, Sarah Meyook, David ArlinJohn, and Peter Meyook for their gum boots and fun spirit; John Carmichael for the fresh fish and stories while out on the river; Tom's family, including Ian, Margo, Ocean, Sam, Jimmy Doug Meyook, Uncle Peter Meyook, and his aga, Sarah Meyook; Charlene Dobmeier and Meaghan Craven from Fifth House for taking on this large project; and especially Tessa Macintosh for her amazing photographs and friendship.

For my dad, who taught me
how to work on the land.

The Delta Is My Home

Ehdııtat shanankat t'agoonch'uu
Uvanga Nunatarmuıtmı aımayuaqtunga

By **TOM McLEOD** *and*
MINDY WILLETT
Photographs by **Tessa Macintosh**

FIFTH HOUSE

Hi,
My name is Tom McLeod. I am eleven years old and in Grade 6. I have a younger sister named Ocean and two older brothers named Ed and Sam. I live in Aklavik, Northwest Territories, in the Mackenzie Delta.

I'm going to tell you about me and my family, our town, the Delta, and what I like to do. I hope you like my stories as the Delta is a special place. It is where I love to hunt and fish and go out on the land. Being on the land with my family is where I get my stories from. It's where I'm most happy.

You should come and visit someday. Until then, here's my story.

Quyannaini and Mahsi' choo.

TOM MCleod

The Delta is my

Mount Goodenough or Chigwaazraii. The area around the mountain has long been used by the people of Aklavik for berry picking, fishing, and hunting caribou, moose, and Dall sheep.

When the river breaks up in the spring, it is an exciting time. Everyone goes out to see the big chunks of ice floating by their community.

home.

This is a peat bog in the bush. There are many habitats in the Delta, from spruce forests in the south to the tundra in the north. This diversity makes the Delta an attractive place for many animal species.

The Delta is large in size and beautiful in detail.

The Mackenzie Delta is the largest delta in Canada. It floods every spring, which makes it very nutrient rich. The flooding also makes the water channels change over time, with new waterways continually being carved out.

My dad's name is Ian. He is *Gwich'in* and is a renewable resource officer, so he works with wildlife. He also is a member of the Gwich'in Land Use Planning Board. He makes sure that people take care of the animals and the land properly. He has taught me how to drive a boat, shoot a gun, and set traps. But most important, he has taught me to respect the land.

To hunt ducks, Tom uses a Winchester 12-gauge shotgun. It is a left-handed model and uses steel shot ammunition. It is now illegal to hunt migratory birds with lead shot because many birds were getting sick from lead poisoning.

Aklavik

"Aklavik" means "place where one gets grizzly bear" in Inuvialuktun (a language of the Inuvialuit). It is located in the northern range of the Gwich'in Settlement Region and the southern lands of the Inuvialuit. The culture of the town is a mix of Gwich'in, Inuvialuit, Métis, and Euro-Canadian people.

My Mom's name is Margo. She is *Inuvialuit*. Since my dad is Gwich'in, that makes me and my brothers and sister mixed. Aklavik is cool that way. About half our town's people are Gwich'in and the other half Inuvialuit. We learn a lot from each other.

Margo is teaching Ocean how to embroider uppers (the top part of moccasins). The most common patterns are flowers.

I'm in Grade 6 at Moose Kerr School here in Aklavik. Our school goes from kindergarten to Grade 12. My favourite class is Computer Science. This winter, an artist came to our class and taught us how to make digital cartoons—I loved it!

The sidewalks at Tom and Ocean's school are boardwalks. In the springtime, even when you're walking on the boardwalks you need to wear your rubber boots!

Velma Illasiak, who is of Gwich'in descent and was born in Aklavik, is the principal at Moose Kerr School. She and others have worked hard to make the school a beautiful place where the students love to learn. This is the library.

Tom and Ocean use the Gwich'in Social and Cultural Institute website to look up traditional stories. Today they're learning about Shìàdii or Shìłee Rock, which is a sacred site on the Peel River above Fort McPherson. Go to www.gwichin.ca to check it out.

I've learned in school that the Delta Braid has become a symbol of our cultural mix. We put this braid on the bottom of our parkas, around our school, on books, everywhere.

Long ago, Gwich'in women used porcupine quills dipped in dyes made out of plants to decorate their clothes. The Inuvialuit used sealskin strips to make designs. Both peoples had geometric shapes in their traditional parkas. Making these fancy clothes must have meant they had a lot of extra time in the day. The women with the fanciest parkas had husbands who were the best hunters. Today, my mom uses bias tape instead of sealskin when she makes a Delta Braid.

The braids really are everywhere! When you come and visit, you'll see what I mean.

Today's parka makers use bias tape to make the Delta Braid. To make a braid you must sew together narrow, overlapping strips of colourful fabrics. By using pieces of contrasting colours, the parka artist develops geometric designs. To finish the parka, the artist often trims it with wolverine fur.

Principal Velma Illatsiak, Korean volunteer Illa Chie, and fifteen-year-old Dustin Lee Edwards painted murals in the lobby to make all the students of the school feel welcome and to celebrate their cultural diversity. Ocean is standing in front of the Gwich'in mural.

7

Sometimes the Delta floods. Since Aklavik is in the Delta, it floods, too.

In the late 1950s, the Canadian government had the "great" idea to move our town to a place where it wouldn't flood. It set up a town just east of here, called Inuvik. The government wanted all the people from Aklavik to move there, but lots of people wouldn't go because they knew and loved the land here. They knew where the best hunting and fishing places were. And they knew that our history is here in the Delta. I guess that's why our town motto is "Never Say Die." We're still here.

From the old rubber outers that protect hand-sewn moccasins to the modern rubber or "gum" boots, the fashion in the Delta is waterproof footwear!

The Aklavik flag with the town's motto, "Never Say Die." It features a muskrat and an open book.

In 2006, we got lots of snow, more than usual. In the spring, the water levels were already high when the ice on the Mackenzie and Peel Rivers broke. The ice got jammed up and our town flooded. A flood hadn't happened since 1992, so this was the first time I saw this happen.

You should have seen it! We were cruisin' through the town in our boat. It was lots of fun.

We had to evacuate about three hundred people. They sent the Elders and little kids to Inuvik. Some people were surrounded by water, and we had to help them get out of their houses by boat. We had to rescue my *aga* that way.

The Delta people live up to their motto. After this photo was taken of Tom helping to evacuate his aga (grandma), Tom's dad took his family duck and muskrat hunting. They found a patch of dry land on which to build a fire, tell jokes, and savour the spoils of their hunt.

During the flood we went hunting. We found dry land and my dad marked a tree with an axe, as the high ground would be a good place to build a cabin one day.

While we were eating, an Elder named John Carmichael pulled up in his boat. He had seen our fire and stopped by for a visit. He also dropped off some fresh whitefish that he had just pulled from his nets. Yummy!

My mom invited him to join us, and soon we were all chatting and catching up on the news. Who had been evacuated? How were we all doing? Where were the ducks and muskrats most plentiful?

John Carmichael shares the news. The northern rivers not only provide food for the people but also act as a sort of "Canada Post," providing the place and the means for friends to catch up.

John lives on the bank of the Peel River in his log home. He chops down wood throughout the spring and summer to make sure he can heat his house in the winter. When you live out on the land you need to work each day to prepare for the following season.

People say I'm a good story teller. Sometimes CBC calls me up and I share stories on the radio. I tell the people in the NWT about my latest trip on the land with my dad.

Tom's aga listens to the story of Tom's first caribou as he tells the listeners of Northwind, a CBC North Radio show that airs all across the NWT during lunch hour.

Our Stories: My First Caribou

I was nine years old when I shot my first caribou. My sister, Ocean, and I stalked a caribou that my dad had accidentally wounded when hunting. We would never leave a wounded animal, even if it took a long time to find it. When we found it, I took a shot. My dad says it was a very good shot considering that the caribou was still moving around a lot. Because my dad taught me, I knew how to be safe with the gun while travelling through the swampy land.

The first caribou that I hunted all on my own was at Canoe Lake about a year later. My parents were running a youth camp and there were caribou about three kilometres behind the cabin. My dad, a school friend, and I walked to go and get one. I shot it from about sixty metres. We had to skin it and carry it all the way back to the camp. It was fun to share the meat with my classmates. I felt very proud of myself.

How Muskrats Make

In the springtime, people really love to go out "ratting" and duck hunting. There are so many muskrats here that Aklavik is called "The Muskrat Capital of Canada." If you haven't seen them before, rats are like small beavers that swim around rivers and lakes eating plants. Muskrats make their homes on the shoreline or riverbank. In the winter, they make breathing holes (called push-ups) so they can travel under the ice to find food. Some push-ups have one or two rooms inside so the muskrats can move from room to room.

My drawing shows how the rats use the push-ups to get food and avoid predators, like foxes.

1. Lake freezes and muskrat chews a hole through the thin ice.

2. Muskrat carries plants and dirt to ice surface.

HELP ME

4. Many muskrats are taken by predators while building push-ups.

5. Push-up is complete but it is not yet froze so the muskrat is still vulnerable to predat

12

Push-ups

3. Muskrat begins to form push-up.

6. Cold and snow combine to secure push-up.

The muskrat is a large, aquatic rodent. Muskrats live in wetlands and are very good swimmers with partially webbed hind feet. They feed on cattails and other aquatic vegetation. Their predators include mink, foxes, lynx, wolves, and large owls.

A muskrat push-up on the Peel River.

Rats are most active at night. When we go hunting, we leave at about midnight and stay up all night. We get our sleep really backward, just like the rats. It's beautiful in the midnight sun. Everything looks orange and pink.

Tom and his family use long skinny wooden stretchers to stretch the rat skins. Then, they hang the skins in the shed until they are dry.

When we come home from hunting rats, my mom skins them, and then we stretch and dry them. We sell most of the furs to the fur buyers who auction them off in North Bay, Ontario. The furs are then used to make coats. Some we keep to make hats or mitts. When I was a kid, my parka was made entirely of rats.

Rat Sunday in the Muskrat Capital of Canada

While furs had always been used for clothing in the North, the fur trade started in Aklavik around 1912. The Hudson's Bay Company started a trading post at the mouth of the Pokiak Channel, where an Inuvialuit campsite was. This post became the town of Aklavik. Because the fur trade grew so much in the area, by 1918, the town expanded across the river to where it is now. In the 1940s, Aklavik was the world centre for a million-dollar trade in muskrat hides.

In 1933, the men in Aklavik placed a different donation on the collection plate at church: muskrat furs!

Tom hunts at midnight. The Arctic Circle (66° 33' N latitude) marks the point where for at least one day in the year the sun remains above the horizon for a full twenty-four hours. Aklavik is located at 68° 13' N latitude, so it is in the "land of the midnight sun." At Aklavik, the sun stays up all night in the summer (from 26 May to 18 July). Of course, the reverse is true in the winter, when the sun does not come up for about one month!

Why do Birds Migrate North in the Summer?

The reason for North-South migration is complicated. The simplest explanation for it is that there is lots of food in the North in the summer. Plants and insects flourish in the long daylight hours. Because birds can fly and thus travel long distances, they can take advantage of the rich food source in the summer and then head south when it gets cooler and the food source is no longer there.

You should see how many birds there are here in the springtime—thousands. They come from the south to nest here. Sometimes I find the nests in the swampy willows. Birds are really fun to watch. I especially like swans—they look so beautiful. Did you know that swans mate for life?

White-winged Scoter   *Surf Scoter*

There are two species of scoters (locally known as black ducks) common in the Delta. These are the white-winged scoter and the surf scoter. Scoters are called "divers" because they dive to capture their food—clams and invertebrates.

The Green-winged teal, with its short neck and small bill, is the smallest North American duck. Ducks Unlimited's youth conservation program, Green Wing, is named after this tiny duck. Go to www.greenwing.org to find out more.

Green-winged Teal

I like to eat all kinds of ducks, but my dad and I don't bother hunting the really small ones like the green-winged teal. We call them "cup-a-soup ducks" because they have so little meat. Black ducks are my favourite to hunt because they are really big and fat and taste so good. My mom is a really good hunter, too. My sister is too young to shoot the gun but she still goes hunting with us.

When we get ducks, my sister and mom pluck them. They do this while we're out in the bush.

Plucking a Duck
Instructions by Ocean

To pluck a duck, you have to start at the chest. While you hold the feet, pull the feathers up toward the duck's head. Then pluck all the way up the neck, then pluck the belly. You have to pluck all the way down to the tail. Pluck the tail feathers, and, finally, pluck the whole back side and under the wings.

When the plucking is done, I singe the remaining feathers over a fire as I smoke the meat. The meat tastes better when it's been smoked.

When I singe ducks, I have to put on gloves to protect my hands. I take the duck by the head and two wings and hold them up to the head, all together. I then tuck the head in between the wings. Then, I take hold of the feet and hold the duck over the fire until the down on the duck has been singed off.

My mom can really cook ducks. My favourite way to eat them is oven roasted. I like to eat them with my mom's bannock. Her bannock is the best under the sun. I don't want to eat anybody else's bread except my mom's and my *aga's*.

Margo first learned how to make bannock when she was six.

A quick tea break. Margo packs about ten bannock pieces in each plastic bag to take out in the boat when the McLeods go hunting.

Our Food: *Bannock*

Margo's Homemade Bread and Bannock

- Put just about half of a 10-pound bag of flour in a bowl. Pour a little bit of milk in with the flour (about 2 tablespoons of milk) and leave it.
- Mix together salt (just a little bit in the middle of your hand), 3½ handfuls of sugar, and 2 tablespoons of yeast. Add a dipper of warm water and let it sit for about 3 minutes. Mix it together to ensure no sugar or salt are on the bottom. Then, pour the yeast mixture into the flour mixture and mix them together. (You might need to add more warm water, but it should not feel too sticky.)
- Then, add 1½ pounds of lard. Mash it up with your hands and mix it up with the bread mixture. Don't melt it.
- Let the dough sit for 2½ hours and let it rise. Put it in pans and let it rise again for half an hour or 45 minutes. Preheat the oven to 350°C before baking.
- Put the bread in the oven for about 30 to 40 minutes, depending on how brown you want to have it.

To make bannock, use the same recipe, but grab small little rounds of dough, spread them out in your hands, make holes with your fingers, and then deep-fry them in a pan with lard. Make sure the lard is really hot before you fry them. Put them in the pan, fry one side until it is golden brown, then turn them over until they're done.

My dad says that there are fewer black ducks now. He says that long ago there used to be many more. Some ducks have bands on them, which are tiny identification tags on their legs. If someone shoots a duck with a band on it, he hands it in to my dad when he is at work. The band number tells my dad about the bird. He can look it up and find out where the bird was banded, and that tells him how far it travelled and how old it is, and stuff like that.

The information my dad gets from the bands is helping to answer questions about ducks in decline. I'm glad people are asking questions. I want to always see ducks around here.

Organizations like the Gwich'in Renewable Resource Board and Ducks Unlimited Canada are trying to figure out why there aren't as many black ducks in the Mackenzie Delta as there used to be.

Northerners have always hunted ducks, muskrats, and other animals for survival. We are careful about how we use the land. To be good hunters, we need to pay attention to what is happening on the land around us—that's why it's important for us to be out on the land. We are the first to know if the land and animals are changing.

At six in the morning we come home from a long night of hunting. Tomorrow night we'll go out again.

Wanna come?

23

All the Details!

Birds in the Mackenzie Delta – Only a few bird species can survive the long cold winters in the Delta, but in the warmer months, tens of thousands of birds depend on the various Delta habitats. Migrating waterfowl take advantage of the abundant water: some stay in the forested ponds and lakes to breed (mallards, scoters, green-winged teal); others make their way as far north as the coastline of the Arctic tundra (snow geese, tundra swans).

Ducks Unlimited Canada (DUC) – conserves wetland habitats across Canada. DUC wants to protect wetland habitat in the western boreal forest because it is important for breeding waterfowl. DUC makes maps of plants and water in the Mackenzie Delta and Mackenzie Valley, and completes bird surveys so people know what habitats are most important to waterfowl. DUC is concerned that the number of scoter and scaup breeding in the boreal forest has dropped by more than 50 per cent since the 1970s. Hunters and Elders in the Mackenzie Delta noticed that there aren't as many black ducks (scoters) as there used to be. To find out why, DUC started a project in 2001 in the Gwich'in Settlement Area. There is very little scientific knowledge about these two species in the NWT, so this research is important to understanding what factors may be contributing to the decline.

Gwich'in – The Gwich'in are one of the most northerly Aboriginal peoples on the North American continent, living at the northwestern limits of the boreal forest. Only the Inuit live farther north. They are part of a larger family of Aboriginal peoples, known as Athapaskans. The Gwich'in signed their land claim in 1993.

Gwich'in Land Use Planning Board (GLUPB) – developed a land use plan that provides for the conservation, development, and use of land, water, and other resources. The plan is particularly devoted to the needs of the Gwich'in people, while considering the needs of all Canadians. Tom's dad, Ian, is a member of the Gwich'in Land Use Planning Board.

Gwich'in Renewable Resource Board (GRRB) – manages wildlife, fish, and forests in the Gwich'in Settlement Area (GSA). The GRRB mission is to conserve and manage renewable resources (animals, trees, and plants) in a sustainable manner to meet the needs of people today and in the future.

Gwich'in Social and Cultural Institute (GSCI) – The GSCI's goals are to document, preserve, and promote the practice of Gwich'in culture, language, traditional knowledge, and values. They have staff and a board that all work together to achieve their goals. The GSCI's guiding principles are:

• Our Elders play a crucial role as teachers.

They are the source of traditional knowledge, history, language, and culture.

- Preservation of and respect for the land are essential to the well-being of our people and our culture.
- Our family history is important to our identity as Gwich'in.
- All Gwich'in have a role to play in keeping the culture alive.
- Cross-cultural understanding and awareness between Gwich'in and non-Gwich'in is essential in building a new respect and understanding in today's global community.

Inuvialuit – The Inuvialuit are Inuit people who live in the western Canadian Arctic region. Most Inuvialuit speak Inuvialuktun, except for the people of Ulukhaktok, who speak Inuinnaqtun. The Inuvialuit signed their land claim in 1984.

Invertebrates – animals that do not have a backbone. All mammals, like people, are vertebrates, as they have a backbone. Animals like snails, clams, insects, and spiders are invertebrates.

Scoters – Tom and his family hunt black ducks, or scoters. There are two different kinds of scoters in this book. See below for information on how to identify them.

- **How to Identify White-winged Scoters**
  The male is black while the female is brown. Both the male and female have big white patches on their wings that are easy to see when they are flying. Surf scoters don't have these white patches. The male has a white crescent under his eye and a yellow bill.

- **How to Identify Surf Scoters**
  The male is all black while the female is brown. The male has a white patch on top of his head and one on the back of his head, which is why some people call them skunk-heads. The male's bill is large, multicoloured, and swollen at the base. The female has white patches on her cheeks and one on the back of her neck, which is another way that you can tell her apart from a female white-winged scoter.

Taiga – the northerly areas before the Arctic treeline at the northern-most part of the boreal forest.

Tundra – beyond the taiga is the tundra, where few trees grow because of low temperatures and a short growing season.

About the Authors and Photographer

Tom McLeod is a Grade 6 student at Moose Kerr School in Aklavik, Northwest Territories. An animated story teller, Tom enjoys transforming his experiences on the land with his family into stories, such as those told in this book. His voice can be heard on CBC Radio North.

Mindy Willett is an educator living in Yellowknife. She enjoys her work in the north so much that she often pinches herself to make sure it's real. When she isn't pinching herself, she can be found paddling or skiing on Great Slave Lake with her young family.

Tessa Macintosh first came north to Cape Dorset in 1974. A few years later she headed to Yellowknife to work as a photographer for the *Native Press* and then the NWT government. She is now a freelance photographer living in Yellowknife. Her favourite experiences are with people out on the land.